STERLING CHILDREN'S BOOKS
New York

An Imprint of Sterling Publishing
387 Park Avenue South
New York, NY 10016

ISBN 978-1-4027-8352-4

Library of Congress Cataloging-in-Publication Data Available

Distributed in Canada by Sterling Publishing
c/o Canadian Manda Group, 165 Dufferin Street
Toronto, Ontario, Canada M6K 3H6
Distributed in the United Kingdom by GMC Distribution Services
Castle Place, 166 High Street, Lewes, East Sussex, England BN7 1XU
Distributed in Australia by Capricorn Link (Australia) Pty. Ltd.
P.O. Box 704, Windsor, NSW 2756, Australia

For information about custom editions, special sales, and premium and corporate
purchases, please contact Sterling Special Sales at 800-805-5489
or specialsales@sterlingpublishing.com.

Printed in China
Lot #:
2   4   6   8   10   9   7   5   3   1
01/13

www.sterlingpublishing.com/kids

SILVER PENNY STORIES

Thumbelina

Told by Kathleen Olmstead
Illustrated by Linda Olafsdottir

There once was a woman who wanted a child. She went to a fairy and asked for help.

"Plant this seed in a flowerpot," the fairy said, "and a child will grow."

The plant grew quickly. A beautiful flower appeared on top. "Such a pretty flower," the woman said.

She kissed the petals, and the flower opened.

A tiny girl—no bigger than half a thumb—was inside the flower. She was very beautiful and wore a yellow dress. The woman called her Thumbelina.

Everyone loved Thumbelina. She played in a bowl of water using a flower petal as a boat. She slept in half a walnut shell. Thumbelina lived a happy life.

One night, a large, ugly, wet toad watched Thumbelina sleep. "She would make a good wife for my son," the toad said.

Quietly, the toad carried away the walnut shell with Thumbelina still sleeping inside it.

The toad and her son put Thumbelina on a lily pad in a stream. "She cannot swim to shore," the toad said. "She will be trapped until she marries you."

In the morning, Thumbelina woke up. She started to cry. "How will I get home?"

She was very scared.

Some fish in the stream heard Thumbelina crying. They came to help. The fish chewed through the stem of the lily pad. Thumbelina was free! She floated downstream on the lily pad.

A beautiful butterfly landed on the lily pad. Thumbelina climbed onto the butterfly's back. It flew away, carrying Thumbelina across the water to the forest floor.

Thumbelina tried to be brave. She missed her mother but did not cry. "I must be strong," she said. "I will send a letter as soon as I can."

Thumbelina lived happily in the forest. She drank honey from petals and water dripping off leaves. She built a little hut in the grass. All was well until winter came.

It was too cold! She wrapped herself in leaves but she could not get warm. Luckily, Thumbelina met a mouse. "You can stay with me," the mouse said.

A mole lived next door to the mouse. "He has a very big home," the mouse said. "He is blind. He would enjoy your stories and songs."

So, every day, Thumbelina walked
through a tunnel to see Mole. She
sang songs and told stories
to entertain him. Soon, Mole fell
in love with Thumbelina, but he
did not tell her.

One day, Thumbelina found a swallow in the tunnel. The bird was very, very sick. "Don't worry," Thumbelina said. "I will take care of you."

Thumbelina cared for the bird all winter. By spring, he was better. "I would have died without you," he said.

Thumbelina waved as the swallow flew away.

Mouse had news for Thumbelina.
"Mole wants to marry you," she said.
"Isn't that wonderful?"

Thumbelina did not want to marry
Mole. She did not love him and did
not want to live underground.

Luckily, the swallow returned. "Come with me, Thumbelina," he said. "I am going south."

Thumbelina climbed on to the swallow's back. They flew away.

The swallow brought Thumbelina to a field of colorful flowers. She looked all around her. A handsome man was standing on the flower next to her. He gave her a beautiful red tulip.

He was the prince of all the flowers. They fell in love right away.

Together, they found Thumbelina's home. And in the forest not far from where she grew up, they lived happily ever after.